# MR AESOP'S STORY SHOP

FOR SU, WITH THANKS   B.H.

FOR ALEX, LILY, AND RUDY   J.S.

Text copyright © 2010 Bob Hartman
Illustrations copyright © 2010 Jago Silver
This edition copyright © 2010 Lion Hudson

The moral rights of the author and illustrator
have been asserted

A Lion Children's Book
an imprint of
**Lion Hudson plc**
Wilkinson House, Jordan Hill Road,
Oxford OX2 8DR, England
www.lionhudson.com
ISBN 978 0 7459 6915 2

First edition 2010
1 3 5 7 9 10 8 6 4 2 0

**Acknowledgments**
I want to thank Laura Gibbs, whose translation of Aesop's fables I worked from in these
retellings, and whose introduction to the life of Aesop provided much of the information
about the storyteller that you will find in this book.

A catalogue record for this book is available
from the British Library

Typeset in 17/20 Lapidary 333 BT
Printed in China August 2010 (manufacturer LH06)

Distributed by:
UK: Marston Book Services Ltd, PO Box 269, Abingdon, Oxon OX14 4YN
USA: Trafalgar Square Publishing, 814 N Franklin Street, Chicago, IL 60610
USA Christian Market: Kregel Publications, PO Box 2607, Grand Rapids, MI 49501

# MR AESOP'S
## STORY SHOP

BOB HARTMAN  ILLUSTRATED BY JAGO

LION
CHILDREN'S

# CONTENTS

# INTRODUCTION

WHEN I BEGAN writing this book, I didn't want to retell the stories without first finding out more about who Aesop was and why his tales are called "fables". I had fun looking for the answers and was surprised by what I discovered about this storyteller.

We know from an ancient Greek historian named Herodotus that Aesop lived on a Greek island called Samos, off the coast of modern Turkey. Herodotus lived over 2,500 years ago and Aesop over a century earlier, so the stories you are about to read have been around for a long, long time!

The little we know about the storyteller comes from a later *Life of Aesop* that was written 600 years after he lived, so it's hard to know how much is true and how much was made up. This writer says that Aesop was an ugly man with a bald head and bandy legs – a description that interested me. He also wrote that Aesop was a slave who was later set free. This set me thinking: I wondered what might have happened if Aesop had started up his own business, running a stall in the *agora* (that's Greek for marketplace), doing what he loved best – entertaining people and telling fables?

And fables? A fable is a particular kind of story that teaches a lesson, has a moral or makes a point. The Greek word for that moral is *epimythium*, which simply means "after the story". And that's exactly where the "moral" usually comes – tagged on at the end of the story so you don't miss the point.

Originally, Aesop's fables were told to adults, memorized by adults, and eventually written down by adults as lessons for how they should live! As you will see, however, the stories have something to say to people of all ages, grown-ups and children alike. I enjoyed finding a new way to retell the fables in this book and I hope you'll enjoy them too!

Bob Hartman

# THE MOUSE AND THE LION

THE SHOPS WERE SHUTTING. THE NOISY CRIES OF THE STALLHOLDERS AND THE CHATTER OF THE CUSTOMERS HAD DIED DOWN AT THE END OF THE DAY. BUT IN ONE CORNER OF THE GREEK MARKETPLACE, UNDER A FADED AWNING, THINGS WERE JUST GETTING STARTED.

A little bald man, with bandy legs and a crooked smile, laid out olives and cheese on a rickety table. And then, in a booming voice that belied his size, he called out to the people as they made their way home.

"My name is Aesop! Once I was a slave. Now I am a free man. I have refreshments to sell and stories to tell. Stop for a moment — and enjoy!"

A little crowd gathered. Men, women, slaves, and children.

"So what kind of stories do you tell?" someone shouted from the back. "Myths? Legends? Adventures?"

"I tell fables," Aesop answered. "Stories with a moral. Stories that make a point."

Then, with a grin and pointing to different people in his audience, the storyteller began.

"You're too small. You're too slow. You're too ugly." And he pulled a silly face that made the children laugh.

"Has anyone ever told *you* that?" he asked. "And then used it to keep you from doing something you really wanted to do?"

Heads nodded. And not just children's heads.

"Well then," Aesop grinned, "perhaps this story is for you.

"Once there was a mouse. A little mouse who lived in the middle of a great big forest.

"One day, the little mouse ran — squeakity squeakity squeak — out of his hole and over a log and under a fallen leaf. He was looking for something to eat.

"But then, suddenly, he stopped. Something big had its paw on the little mouse's tail."

"A cat!" shouted one of the children. "It was a cat."

"It was a kind of cat," said Aesop. "A very big kind of cat."

"A lion!" shouted another child.

"Well done," Aesop nodded. "The lion picked up the little mouse and dangled him over his open mouth.

" 'You're not very big,' he growled, 'but you'll make a lovely little snack.'

" 'Please don't eat me, Big Lion!' the mouse squeaked. 'I promise that if you let me go, I'll… I'll… I'll come back to help you one day!' "

One of the children laughed. "That's silly. A mouse can't help a lion."

"That's exactly what the lion thought," agreed Aesop.

" 'Don't be ridiculous!' the lion roared. 'You're just a little mouse. How could you possibly help me?' The lion paused and then he said, 'But you are small. And you are rather cheeky. So I'll let you go this time. But if you come by here again, I'll gobble you up, I promise!'

" 'All right, Big Lion,' said the little mouse. And – squeakity squeakity squeak – he ran off into the forest.

"The next morning, when the lion woke up, he gave a great big lion yawn. He gave a great big lion stretch. And then, because he was hungry, he gave a great big lion roar."

Then Aesop roared as well – his mouth open so wide that the audience could see all his teeth – well, the ones that were still there!

"And with that," Aesop continued, "the lion leaped from his cave. One lion leap. Two lion leaps. But when he leaped the third time, the lion leaped right into a hunter's trap!

"The ropes wrapped tightly around him. He could hardly move. The more he struggled, the tighter they got. And worse still, he could hear the hunter coming through the forest.

" 'Oh, no!' thought the lion. 'The hunter is going to get me!'

"And then the lion heard something else. Can you guess what that was?" asked Aesop.

"The mouse!" squeaked one of the children.

"Exactly! There he was, sitting on the lion's nose.

" 'Hello, Big Lion!' he squeaked. 'I said that if you let me go, I would come back to help you one day. And today is the day!'

" 'But how can you help?' said the lion. 'The ropes are wrapped tightly around me. I can hardly move. What can you possibly do?'

" 'You'll see,' said the little mouse. And then, squeakity squeakity squeak, he ran up the lion's face, through his hairy mane, and down onto his strong shoulders. The little mouse put his paws around the rope and he opened his little mouth – and there were two rows of sharp little teeth.

"First the mouse nibbled on the rope. Then he chewed on the rope.

Then he gnawed on the rope. And, finally, he opened wide his little mouse mouth and – snap – bit through the rope!

"'Done it!' he squeaked.

"And with the rope bitten through, all the lion had to do was to stretch his big muscles and all the ropes fell off. The lion roared and, with the little mouse hanging from his mane, he leaped back through the forest and into his cave.

"When the lion was safely home, he held the mouse in his paw.

"'Little mouse,' he said, 'you told me that you could help and I did not believe you. But today you saved my life. So now I will let you go, and I promise that you need never worry about me eating you again.'

"'Thank you, Big Lion,' said the little mouse.

"'Goodbye, Big Lion,' he added. And then – squeakity squeakity squeak – the little mouse ran off into the forest. The end!"

The crowd clapped. Aesop bowed. And as everyone left, he smiled and said, "Don't let anyone judge you by the way you look. Remember, even the smallest among us can do amazing things."

EVEN THE SMALLEST CREATURE
DESERVES RESPECT.

# THE CROW AND THE JAR

THE CROWDS WERE STREAMING OUT OF THE MARKETPLACE, THEIR SHOPPING DONE FOR THE DAY. BUT AESOP WAS BUSY, SO BUSY HE WAS SWEATING. BIT BY BIT HE PUSHED AND PULLED AND WIGGLED A HEAVY STONE JAR TO THE MIDDLE OF HIS STALL.

When everything was ready, he called, "My name is Aesop! Once I was a slave. Now I am a free man. I have refreshments to sell and stories to tell. Stop for a moment – and enjoy!"

An audience gathered slowly and when they had sat themselves down, he began.

"Look at my bald head!" he said. "Look how shiny it is! I've been working. I've been sweating. Struggling to move this big, heavy jar. See, it's got a wide bottom and a skinny neck: a bit like me!"

Everyone laughed.

"But I am here to tell you that there are sometimes better ways to do something hard. You don't need to use the muscles in your arms and legs, but the muscle in your head. Your brain!"

And then Aesop began his story:

"Once there was a crow. A very thirsty crow. The crow searched and searched for water to quench his thirst. But because the weather had been hot and dry, he couldn't find even one drop.

"And then the crow spotted a stone jar. A stone jar that looked much like this one. A jar with a wide bottom and a tall thin neck.

"The crow peered into the jar and, sure enough, down at the very bottom, he saw the faintest glimmer of water! Delighted, the crow stuck his beak into the jar. But the neck was much too narrow and the crow's beak much too short for him to reach the water below.

"So the crow tried something else. He banged at the jar and kicked at the

jar and ran at the jar and tried with all his might to push the jar over, hoping that some water would spill out and he could have a drink.

"But try as he might, no amount of pushing or shoving or brute strength could shift that jar.

"The crow was frustrated and exhausted and thirstier than ever. But he was also clever enough to see that he needed to try a different course. And so he stopped. And he thought. And as he did, he spied a pebble on the ground."

Aesop looked at his audience.

"Do you have any pebbles?" he asked them.

They all shook their heads. "No!"

"Then you must find some!" Aesop grinned. "Go now, up and down the street. Bring me as many pebbles as you can gather."

Everyone hesitated, looking at one another, wondering who would go first.

"We can't finish the story until we have pebbles," Aesop explained. "So you'd better hurry."

Some of the children leaped to their feet. And then a few more. And just a few moments later, they raced back to the stall, their hands dirty and overflowing with pebbles.

"Dump them on the floor there, beside the jar," Aesop said. Then he picked up one of the pebbles. He held it between his forefinger and his thumb and he said, "The crow picked up a pebble in his beak. Just like this." And sure enough, that's what Aesop's hand looked like — a crow with a pebble in its beak.

"Then he dropped the pebble in the jar with a *kerplunk*."

And that's what Aesop did.

"Then he dropped in another pebble," Aesop explained.

And Aesop dropped another pebble in the jar.

"Why don't you have a go?" he said to the children. "Go on, take turns. Drop them in one by one."

And so the children did, laughing and racing to see who could drop in the most.

"Finally," said Aesop, "the water rose so high that when the crow dipped his beak into the jar, he was able to drink as much water as he wanted."

And with that, Aesop stuck his finger-beak into the jar — and when he pulled it out, it was wet!

"See?" he grinned.

And everyone cheered.

"Good story!" someone called.

"Even better trick," called someone else.

"It's not just a trick," smiled Aesop. "What the crow did was the most sensible thing in the world. He thought about the problem he had to solve and didn't just use his brute strength. Do the same, and you can accomplish some amazing things, as well!"

BRAINS ARE SOMETIMES
BETTER THAN BRUTE STRENGTH.

# THE FOX AND THE GRAPES

Aesop was just about to start his story. Everyone was settled down in front of his little storytelling stall when an almighty row erupted from the pottery seller's stall next door.

"I saw it first!" shouted a large woman.

"But I had my hand on it!" a smaller lady shouted back.

"Doesn't matter. It's mine now!" said the first woman, grabbing the pot by one of its handles and hoisting it in the air.

"Not if I take it away from you!" growled the second woman, grabbing the other handle.

"Ladies! Ladies!" cried the pottery seller. "Calm down! There are plenty more pots here."

"Not as nice as this one!" shouted the first woman, pulling on the handle now with all her might.

"Nowhere near as nice!" grunted the second woman, pulling just as hard.

Everyone was watching now.

"This is even better than a story, I'd say," chuckled Aesop to one of the children. "But I bet it ends badly."

And so it did.

The pot went this way and that way and back this way again, each woman pulling with all her might.

And then, with a snap, both handles came off, and the pot fell with a crash to the floor.

"Look what you did!" shouted the large woman.

"Me? It was your fault!" the smaller woman shouted back.

"Well, someone is going to have to pay for it!" the pottery seller complained.

"Not me!" grunted the first woman. "She's the one who broke it." And she stormed off.

"It wasn't that nice, anyway!" grumbled the second woman, glancing down at the broken bits. "There are far nicer pots at the shop down the street." And she stormed off as well, turning to the crowd and adding, "Well, what are you looking at?"

"Sour grapes," Aesop answered, though she was already too far away to hear him. "That's what we're looking at."

"Grapes?" asked one of the children at the front. "There weren't any grapes. Just pots."

"Ah, but there are grapes in my story," Aesop grinned. "And, as you will see, the story is all about that pot!"

The audience looked up expectantly.

"Once there was a fox," Aesop began. "A red fox. A sly fox. A proud fox. As the fox walked along one day, she wandered under a grapevine and, happening to look up, spied the most mouth-watering bunch of purple grapes. The fox wanted those grapes. She wanted them so badly she could taste them. But the grapes were hanging high above her head and sadly she could not reach them.

"Now, foxes are good at many things. They are clever. They are quick. They are crafty. But foxes cannot climb. Not trees. Not hedges. And not grapevines either.

"The fox tried. She wanted the grapes so badly. So she began to jump. Up and down. Higher and higher each time – but never high enough to grab even one of those delicious grapes. All she managed to do was to graze her fox nose and tear her fox fur.

"Finally, the fox collapsed – sweaty and frustrated and bruised. And that's when she heard a little voice – squeaking and giggling for all it was worth.

" 'Looks like somebody is going home hungry today,' chirruped a mouse – a little mouse who had been watching all along.

" 'I don't know what you're talking about,' snapped the proud fox, shaking herself and leaping to her feet. 'Those grapes? Those grapes are sour. I wouldn't eat them even if they were sitting right here in front me.'

"And with that, she stuck her nose in the air and strutted off.

"Grapes. Pots," said Aesop. "It's all the same. When people can't have what they want, they pretend they never wanted it in the first place."

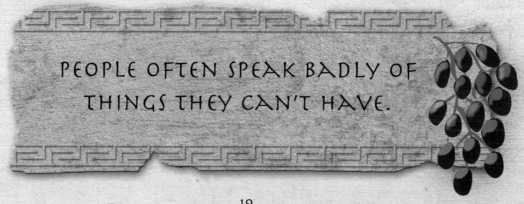

PEOPLE OFTEN SPEAK BADLY OF
THINGS THEY CAN'T HAVE.

# THE CITY MOUSE AND THE COUNTRY MOUSE

THE TRADERS IN THE MARKETPLACE SHOUTED OUT ACROSS THE CROWD.

"Grapes! I have grapes for sale!"

"Cabbages. Get your cabbages here!"

"Chickens! Fresh chickens today."

"Pots! Best pots in the land!"

Bandy-legged and bald-headed, Aesop shouted too – from his stall at the market's edge.

"Peace!" he cried. "Peace of mind for sale! An end to all your worries!"

"Ridiculous!" someone shouted.

"I don't believe it!" called someone else.

"But it's true," Aesop grinned. "And it's guaranteed. Peace of mind. All you need do is listen to my story."

The crowd packed into the space before his stall. Children in front, adults squeezed in behind. And then Aesop began.

"I know what worries you," he said, grinning at the children. "School!" And he made a face and they all giggled.

"Finding the best bargain," he continued, looking at the ladies with their loaded shopping baskets.

"But there is one thing that worries everyone," he concluded. "Money! And that is because everyone wants to be rich."

And all heads nodded.

"Well, I have the answer to your money worries," he announced. "And I am in the perfect position to say this because I am the richest man in Greece!"

"Rubbish!" someone shouted.

"Look at that poor excuse for a stall," someone else chuckled.

"You may laugh," Aesop grinned. "But what I say is true. Listen.

"Once there were two mice, one brown, one grey. The grey mouse lived in the city in the home of a wealthy family. And the brown mouse lived with poor farmers out in the country.

"The city mouse went to visit the country mouse and the country mouse treated the city mouse to a simple meal of acorns. Acorn tarts. Acorn stew. Acorn pie. And a sweet acorn pudding too!"

"Ugh!" grimaced one of the children.

"That's just how the city mouse reacted!" grinned Aesop. "And that

is why, before the meal was even finished, he gave the country mouse an invitation. He asked him to come back to the city with him — to sample the fine food he was used to eating in the rich family's house.

"The country mouse wasn't keen. He liked acorns, he enjoyed all the other simple food he ate, and he was happy living in the farmer's home. But the city mouse wouldn't give up. He asked, then begged, and then pleaded. And, finally, the country mouse agreed.

"The journey was long and tiring, but when they arrived at last and the country mouse saw the delicious food sitting on the rich family's table, all his weariness left him.

"His eyes danced from treat to treat. Fat cheese tarts. Thick lamb stew. Crusty meat pie. And plates full of sticky honey puddings.

"The country mouse couldn't wait! He scrambled up a table leg and scurried around the table top from one scrumptious morsel to another. The city mouse joined him, of course, and through mouthfuls of food

explained that every meal would be like this one!

"Suddenly, the family butler walked into the room.

"The city mouse saw him at once and, quick as a mouse, he ran down a table leg and into the nearest mouse hole.

"But the country mouse was taken completely by surprise. And because he did not know the house, he did not know where to run. Would the man see him? Where should he go? What if there was a cat? He managed to climb down from the table but was left to dash frantically across the floor, looking desperately for a place to hide.

"When at last the butler left, the city mouse crawled out of his hole and went back to his meal.

" 'Come back! There's plenty!' he assured his friend.

"But all the country mouse could do was to sit in a corner trembling.

" 'Eat? At a time like this? I couldn't possibly,' he squeaked. 'What if that man comes back?'

" 'What if he does?' the city mouse shrugged. 'Where else will you find a meal like this?'

" 'I don't know,' the country mouse admitted. 'And I don't care. This is indeed the most amazing food I have ever tasted. But I would rather enjoy a simple meal of acorns in peace than fret and fear and worry over the finest feast.'

"And with that, he went back to his country home, never to return."

Then Aesop bowed and the crowd applauded.

"Do you see?" Aesop smiled, pointing to his rickety market stall. "At heart, I am a country mouse. I may not have much but I am satisfied with my stall and my stories. Satisfied with what I have.

"I don't worry. I don't fret. I have everything I need. And if I have everything I need, I am indeed the richest man in Greece!"

IT IS BETTER TO BE POOR AND SATISFIED THAN RICH AND WORRIED.

# THE ANT AND THE DUNG BEETLE

Word about Aesop's stories was spreading. So the crowd was particularly large one day — the crowd that had crowded around Aesop's little storytelling stall.

They had squeezed in at the front and at the back and at the sides — so squeezed in that when one little girl shifted in her place to make herself more comfortable, she shifted right into Aesop's table full of refreshments and knocked a pile of cakes onto the floor.

She looked as if she was about to cry but Aesop smiled and reassured her. "Not a problem! Those weren't my best cakes anyway." Then he shuffled around the back of the stall and produced a whole new pile.

"These are much better!" he smiled again, setting them on the table. "You see, you have to be prepared for anything!"
Aesop chuckled. "And that reminds me of a story. A story about an ant and a dung beetle."

"What's dung?" asked one of the children.

"What's dung?" grinned Aesop mischievously. "It's poo!"

"Poo!" said the child. "Ewww!"

"It's disgusting, I know," Aesop admitted. "But not to dung beetles. If you're a dung beetle, that's where you find your dinner."

And everyone else went "Ewww!" too.

"Once there was an ant," Aesop continued. "An ant who worked hard, every single day, preparing for winter. Back and forth he would carry the food he collected — bits of fruit and vegetable and meat — from the places he found it to the place, deep in his anthill, where it was stored.

"Every day, he would pass a dung beetle sitting happily in a pile of dung. And, every day, the dung beetle would poke fun at him.

" 'You must be the saddest creature in the world!' the dung beetle would shout. 'Running here and there all day — with no time for fun!'

"At other times, he would call out, 'You are so boring, Ant! Stop. Rest. Enjoy yourself!'

"Or he would snigger and say, 'Stupid ant! You'll work yourself to death!'

"And sometimes he would just lean back on his elbows in the dung and shake his head and laugh.

"The ant, however, never answered back. He never argued. He never complained. In fact, he paid no attention at all to the dung beetle and simply carried on with his work.

"At last, winter came — and with it the winter rains.

"The ant was warm and dry in his anthill and he had plenty of food. But the heavy rain washed all the dung away and the dung beetle was left with nothing. Nowhere to sit and nothing to eat.

"So the dung beetle went to visit the ant. 'Give me some of the food you stored,' he pleaded.

"But the ant shook his head sadly and said, 'No. If you had spent your summer gathering and storing as I did, you would have plenty. But instead you wasted your time making fun of me. And so now you have nothing at all.'"

"That wasn't very nice of the ant," grumbled one of the children.

"I suppose not," Aesop nodded. "But then the fable's not about kindness – it's about 'being prepared' and 'planning for the future' and 'doing what's important'. You see, you can't always count on kindness."

And then he looked at the little girl, picked up a cake, and handed it to her. And she took a big bite and smiled.

"But I have to admit that, when you find it, it's awfully sweet!"

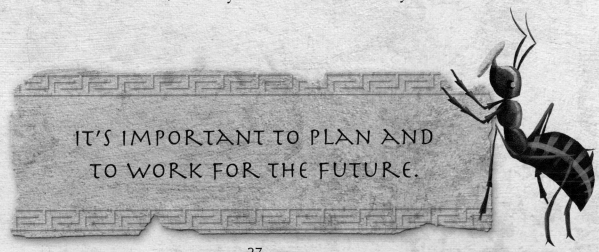

IT'S IMPORTANT TO PLAN AND
TO WORK FOR THE FUTURE.

# THE FOX AND THE RAVEN

THE CROWD CLAPPED AND CHEERED AS AESOP WALKED OUT FROM BEHIND HIS LITTLE STORYTELLING STALL.

"Tell us a story!" someone shouted.

"We love your stories!" called someone else.

"You are the best storyteller in all of Greece!" someone said.

"You flatter me!" Aesop answered. And he bowed and he smiled. And then, suddenly, his smile disappeared and he continued, "But flattery can be a dangerous thing – as I hope my little fable will demonstrate.

"Once there was a raven," he began, "who grabbed a tasty piece of cheese from a market stall – a stall much like this one!

"He flew as fast as he could to his favourite tree. But, along the way, he was spotted by a clever fox, who fancied that tasty piece of cheese for himself.

"The cheese, however, was in the raven's beak. The raven was perched on the highest branch of the tree. And the hungry fox was on the ground, far below.

"Now, as I have

explained before, foxes are good at many things but climbing up trees is not one of them. So the fox needed to find a way to make the cheese come down to him.

"He walked slowly around the tree, thinking. And the raven watched him, amused.

"Finally, the fox stopped. He looked up through the branches and called, 'Raven! I believe you are the most handsome bird I have ever seen.'

"'Handsome?' thought the raven. 'Hmmm.' And he cocked his head to hear what else the fox might say.

"The fox did not disappoint him.

" 'Furthermore,' the fox continued, 'your feathers are so shiny and silky smooth that you must be the envy of every other bird in the sky!'

"The raven liked this. He really did! He had no idea that he was so attractive.

"And then the fox sighed. 'Is it possible,' he asked, 'that you have a voice to match your looks? A singing voice that puts every other bird to shame?'

" 'A singing voice? thought the raven. But he didn't think hard and he didn't think long. The raven so wanted to impress the flattering fox that he forgot he could not sing at all. And even worse, he forgot about what he was holding in his beak.

"The raven opened his mouth and, along with the most horrible squawk, out came his piece of cheese. It fell to the ground and was picked up at once by the fox.

" 'So you do have a voice,' the fox grinned. 'Too bad you don't have a brain to go with it!'

"Then he gobbled the cheese up in one bite and skipped off happily into the woods."

His story finished, Aesop bowed again. And again his audience cheered.

"Bravo, Aesop!"

"Great story, Aesop!"

"Thank you," said Aesop. "So be careful. Careful that what others say doesn't go to your head."

And then he grinned. "Unless, of course, it's true!"

DON'T BE DECEIVED BY FLATTERY.

# THE WOLF IN SHEEP'S CLOTHING

"Drama — today!" called Aesop. "Come one. Come all. Come and see the Actors!"

The crowd pushed and shoved its way in front of Aesop's little storytelling stall. This was something different!

And when everyone had found a place to stand or to sit or to squeeze in, Aesop held two masks up high.

"Tragedy!" he shouted as he held up a frowning mask.

"Comedy!" he continued, a grinning mask in his other hand.

"So where are the actors?" someone shouted back.

"The actors?" Aesop answered. "The actors are all around. You are the actors!"

Two or three people booed.

"Hear me out," Aesop replied in a flash. "We are all actors from time to time, when we pretend to be something we are not. We want to impress someone, so we pretend to be smarter than we are, or richer or braver or stronger. Sometimes, no harm is done. But at other times, we make things very difficult for ourselves, as you will see.

"Once there was a wolf — a lazy wolf but a clever wolf — who had grown tired of chasing sheep.

"'Running uphill, running downhill,' he sighed. 'It might build up the appetite but it wears me out. There must be a better way to get my dinner.'

"And then, one evening, as he lay at the edge of the woods and watched the shepherd lead his flock into the sheepfold, he tried to find an answer to his problem.

"'If I could get in the sheepfold with the sheep,' he thought, 'there would be no place for them to run. I could catch them with no effort at all. And then I could eat until I burst! But how to get in without the shepherd spotting me?'

"The wolf dozed off as he thought. And as he dozed, he dreamed. Of sheep and wolves. And wolves and sheep. And when he awoke, he had his idea!

"'A wolf and a sheep,' he thought. 'A wolf dressed as a sheep! What better way to get into the sheepfold than to pretend to be a sheep myself?'

"So the wolf found himself a sheepskin and dressed himself up as a sheep.

"And then, his disguise complete, he crept out of the woods. Slowly, he approached the flock. Closer and closer he crept. And, finally, he mingled right in with them.

"He baaed when they baaed, which he found quite amusing. He chewed on the grass when they did, which he found quite disgusting. None of the real sheep seemed to pay him any attention. So when the shepherd led the flock into the sheepfold that evening, the wolf just tripped along with the rest.

"He watched patiently as the sheep settled down for the night, and he waited quietly as the baaing turned to snoring.

"The wolf was terribly hungry by now. And happier than he had ever been, for a feast lay spread out before him! His plan was perfect. And now he would reap the rewards!

"And then the wolf saw a flash of something out of the corner of his eye. Something long and sharp, gleaming in the moonlight.

"You see, the wolf was not alone. Someone else was hungry. And that someone was the shepherd. Into the sheepfold he walked, knife in hand, ready to kill a sheep for his supper.

"The wolf's disguise was good. Too good as it happens. For when the shepherd plunged his knife into a sheep, it was the wolf he killed. What a surprise it was for both of them!"

"Ugh!" said one of the children. "So the shepherd ate the wolf?"

Aesop laughed. "I hope not! In fact, I'm sure he didn't. But I suspect he learned a lesson that came too late for the wolf: that it can sometimes be very dangerous to wear a mask – to pretend to be something you're not!"

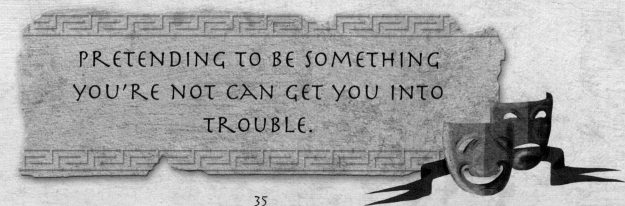

PRETENDING TO BE SOMETHING
YOU'RE NOT CAN GET YOU INTO
TROUBLE.

# THE DOG AND THE RIVER

THE PEOPLE WERE GATHERED IN FRONT OF AESOP'S STORYTELLING STALL. THEY WERE EATING, THEY WERE DRINKING, THEY WERE READY TO LISTEN TO HIS LATEST STORY. AND THEN, ALL OF A SUDDEN, A DOG CAME RUSHING OUT OF NOWHERE. AND AENEAS, THE BUTCHER, CAME RUSHING AFTER IT.

"Come back here!" Aeneas shouted. "Give me my meat!"

The dog ducked into the crowd, a steak between its teeth. And Aeneas barged in after it, pushing and shoving and bulling his way through.

Drinks were spilled. Cakes dropped. And one or two of Aesop's audience ended up on the ground. But the butcher never caught the dog and the last the crowd saw of him, he was sweating and swearing and chasing the four-legged thief down the street.

"Is everyone all right?" Aesop asked when the butcher and the dog had gone.

"A bruise or two back here!" someone called. "But nothing serious."

Aesop nodded his head. "Good." And then he smiled and said, "I was going to tell you another story. But I think this one might be more appropriate.

"Once there was a dog — a greedy dog — who stole a piece of meat from a butcher's stall. And when he had escaped the butcher, much like that dog will surely escape from my friend Aeneas, he came to a river.

"Now, this was not a roaring river, nor even a fast-flowing one. No, the water in this river was relatively still, so when the dog passed, he caught sight of his reflection.

"You know as well as I do that water has a way of distorting whatever is reflected in it. It makes things larger or smaller or wobblier, depending upon the angle and the light.

"In this case, the meat that the dog saw reflected in the water looked much bigger than the meat he had in his mouth. He wanted that bigger piece. He really did. He wanted it badly. So badly, in fact, that he dropped the piece of meat he already had and leaped into the water after the new piece!

"The dog was disappointed, of course. There was no meat in the water. And worse still, when he climbed out, wet and cold, and went to pick up the piece he had dropped, a raven swooped down from the sky and snatched it away in its claws.

"And so the dog walked home, sad and soggy but somewhat wiser. For he had learned that wanting more sometimes leaves you with nothing at all."

"Do you think that our dog will learn that?" asked one of the children.

"Probably not," Aesop smiled. "But our friend Aeneas might. Look, here he is now."

Staggering and sweating, Aeneas waved a tired hand in front of his face.

"I know. I know," he gasped. "I should have let it go. It was only a piece of meat. And now – the mess I have made. I am so sorry. Let me make it up to you, Aesop. Drinks, cakes! They're all on me!"

"See!" Aesop smiled, as the children rushed forward for their treats. "Aeneas has learned his lesson. And we get the benefit. Oh, and one cake only, children. We don't want to be greedy, do we?"

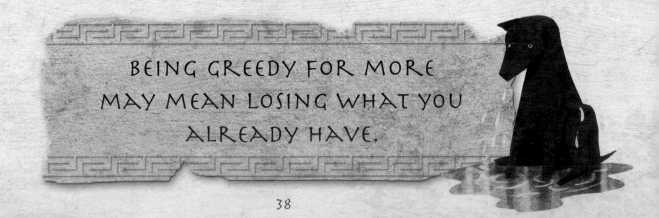

BEING GREEDY FOR MORE
MAY MEAN LOSING WHAT YOU
ALREADY HAVE.

# THE TORTOISE AND THE HARE

THE CROWDS GATHERED, AS USUAL, BEFORE AESOP'S LITTLE STORYTELLING STALL. CHILDREN AT THE FRONT, ADULTS BEHIND. BUT AESOP WAS NOT HIS USUAL NOISY SELF.

He did not shout. He did not call. He just stood there glumly, rubbing his bald head and looking sad and forlorn.

"I have broken a pot," he said, at last.

And someone in the crowd said, "Aww."

"A little more sympathy, if you please," Aesop begged.

And a few more voices "Awwed" along.

"It was my best pot!" he insisted.

And now everyone joined in. "Aww!"

"But all is not lost," Aesop smiled. "For I have managed to salvage two pieces of my broken pot. And with them I intend to prove that with a little perseverance you can make something good out of any situation — and that you can find a story *anywhere*!"

He held up the first piece.

"Can anyone tell me what this looks like?" he asked.

"A broken piece of pottery!" chuckled someone at the back.

"Anyone else?" Aesop sighed. "Someone at the front, perhaps."

"It looks like a tortoise," said one of the children.

"Thank you," Aesop smiled. Then he held up another piece. "And how about this one?"

"A hare!" called out another child. "It looks like a hare."

"So it does," said Aesop. "And so our story begins – with a tortoise and wa hare.

"The hare was quick," said Aesop, "as hares usually are. And the tortoise? Well, the tortoise was not quick. In fact, he was painfully and ploddingly slow.

"The hare was laughing at the tortoise one day," Aesop continued. "Making fun of his plodding tortoise feet and his toddling tortoise pace. So the tortoise did something rather reckless. He told the hare – slowly and methodically, of course – that he could beat him in a race."

"A race?" laughed someone in the crowd. "The tortoise could never win!"

"That's exactly what the hare thought," Aesop nodded.

" 'Words are one thing. Actions another,' the hare sneered. And he accepted the tortoise's challenge right then and there.

"Together, they decided that the fox should set the course and umpire the event because she was the cleverest animal of them all.

"And when the agreed date arrived, all the animals lined up to watch.

" 'Ready. Steady. Go!' barked the fox.

"The tortoise took off at once, plodding along as fast as his stumpy legs would carry him. Which, of course, was not very fast at all!

"And the hare?"

"The hare raced to the finish line in a flash!" shouted one of the children. "Winner!"

"You would think so," Aesop nodded. "But the hare was so confident of his natural abilities – his quickness and his speed – that he did not take the tortoise seriously. So instead of racing for the finish, he lay down at the

starting line and went to sleep.

"The tortoise plodded, the hare snored.

"The tortoise plodded, the hare snored.

"The tortoise plodded, the hare snored – the whole of that long afternoon.

"And when the hare at last awoke and saw the sun setting in the sky, then and only then did he join the race. His legs were strong. His feet were fast. And just as he crested the hill that led to the final stretch, he caught a glimpse of the cheering animal crowd.

"But they weren't cheering for him. No, they were cheering for the tortoise, who had plodded on and on and who had stepped, finally and first, across the finish line!"

"Didn't see that coming!" someone shouted.

"No," Aesop chuckled. "And neither did the hare!"

Then he held the broken pottery pieces high.

"But it's not always the one with the natural ability that succeeds. Sometimes it's the one who sticks to it and does the best with what he has."

STICKING TO YOUR GOALS MAY
BRING MORE SUCCESS THAN BEING
LAZY WITH YOUR TALENTS.

# THE WOLF AND THE DOG

Aesop called out to the crowd, called out as the people passed his little storytelling stall.

"My name is Aesop! Once I was a slave. Now I am a free man. I have refreshments to sell and stories to tell. Stop for a moment — and enjoy!"

And so they stopped, as usual. And when they had sampled Aesop's cakes and juices, one of the children asked, "Why are there so many animals in your stories?"

Aesop smiled. "The answer is simple," he explained. "We see ourselves in the animals. Some of us are like bulls — powerful and strong. Some are like ants — busy and industrious. Others are like pigs — greedy, their noses always

in the trough. As for me, I fancy myself as a wolf."

Someone at the back laughed right out loud. "A wolf? You look more like a chicken!"

"Or a goose!" someone added.

"Or a hairless squirrel!" suggested someone else.

Aesop laughed along with the crowd.

"Well observed!" he chuckled. "But I'm not talking about what a person looks like on the outside. I'm talking about what they are like within. I am a wolf. I really am. And I hope this story will make that clear."

He looked around to see that he had everyone's attention. Then he cleared his throat and began.

"The wolf and the dog met, one moonlit night, at the edge of a farmyard. They could not have been more different.

"The wolf was hungry. The dog well fed.

"The wolf's fur was matted and torn. The dog's silky coat was shiny and groomed.

"The wolf was tired, worn out from chasing after his dinner. The dog was rested and calm.

"The wolf was thin and gaunt. The dog was plump and cheerful.

" 'So how are you on this lovely evening?' asked the dog.

" 'Lovely?' growled the wolf. 'Lovely for some. Not so lovely when you are tired and hungry.'

" 'I wouldn't know about that,' the dog smiled contentedly. 'I have everything I need here.'

" 'And how is that?' the wolf grunted.

" 'It's all thanks to the man,' the dog barked. 'When I am hungry, he feeds me. When I am tired, he gives me a soft bed to sleep on. When I want to play, he tosses me a stick or a ball. And when I am cold, he lets me sit in front of his fire.'

" 'Sounds wonderful,' said the wolf with a sigh – a deep sigh, because he was more than a little jealous.

" 'It is!' said the dog. 'In fact, if you like, I could tell the man about you. We can always use a little extra help around the farmyard.'

" 'Really?' said the wolf. 'You would do that for me?'

" 'Absolutely,' said the dog. 'But it will have to wait until morning.'

" 'Because the man is asleep?' asked the wolf.

" 'No, because of the chain,' the dog answered. 'I can only go so far, you see. And the chain doesn't reach to the house.'

"The wolf looked more closely. There was, indeed, a chain, attached at one end to a post hammered into the ground and at the other end to a collar around the dog's neck.

" 'I see,' said the wolf. 'A collar. A chain. So you are the man's slave, then?'

" 'Yes, well, you could put it that way,' said the dog.

" 'Then you can keep your fine food,' the wolf grunted. 'And your soft bed and your sticks and your balls and your warm fire. None of them is worth the price of my freedom.'

"And with that, the wolf turned tail and ran off into the forest, still tired and hungry but free.

"Do you see?" Aesop grinned. "I once was a slave — another man's possession, like a dog with a chain around his neck. But now I am a free man — free to run my shop and tell my stories. Now I am a wolf!"

FREEDOM IS BETTER THAN ANY
COMFORT OR TREASURE.